Put Beginning Readers on the Right Track with
ALL ABOARD READING™

The All Aboard Reading series is especially designed for beginning readers. Written by noted authors and illustrated in full color, these are books that children really want to read—books to excite their imagination, expand their interests, make them laugh, and support their feelings. With fiction and nonfiction stories that are high interest and curriculum-related, All Aboard Reading books offer something for every young reader. And with four different reading levels, the All Aboard Reading series lets you choose which books are most appropriate for your children and their growing abilities.

Picture Readers

Picture Readers have super-simple texts, with many nouns appearing as rebus pictures. At the end of each book are 24 flash cards—on one side is a rebus picture; on the other side is the written-out word.

Station Stop 1

Station Stop 1 books are best for children who have just begun to read. Simple words and big type make these early reading experiences more comfortable. Picture clues help children to figure out the words on the page. Lots of repetition throughout the text helps children to predict the next word or phrase—an essential step in developing word recognition.

Station Stop 2

Station Stop 2 books are written specifically for children who are reading with help. Short sentences make it easier for early readers to understand what they are reading. Simple plots and simple dialogue help children with reading comprehension.

Station Stop 3

Station Stop 3 books are perfect for children who are reading alone. With longer text and harder words, these books appeal to children who have mastered basic reading skills. More complex stories captivate children who are ready for more challenging books.

In addition to All Aboard Reading books, look for All Aboard Math Readers™ (fiction stories that teach math concepts children are learning in school) and All Aboard Science Readers™ (nonfiction books that explore the most fascinating science topics in age-appropriate language).

All Aboard for happy reading!

For Jane O'Connor, a constant inspiration—W.C.L.

For Shawn Michael Gordon—J.S.

Library of Congress Cataloging-in-Publication Data is available.

ISBN 978-0-448-42472-9   S T

Princess Buttercup

A Flower Princess Story

By Wendy Cheyette Lewison
Illustrated by Jerry Smath

Grosset & Dunlap • New York

In the magic garden,
six Flower Princesses
open their eyes.
Wake up, wake up!
It is the first day of spring!

There is going to be a party.
Princess Lily and Princess Tulip
set the table.

Princess Rose gets
the band ready.

Princess Hyacinth makes a cake.

Princess Iris makes up
a game to play
at the party.

But where is Princess Buttercup?

Princess Buttercup is
out picking buttercups.
One buttercup here.
Two buttercups there.
Now she has lots of buttercups
for the party.

Look!

It is a butterfly.

"How pretty!" she says.

She follows the butterfly.

She forgets all about
the buttercups.
She forgets all about the party.

The butterfly hops
from flower to flower.

Princess Buttercup skips after it.

She looks around.
Where is the butterfly?
And where is she?

Oh, no!

She is in the woods.

And she is lost.

15

But the butterfly is not lost.

It is still looking for flowers.

Princess Buttercup has an idea.

She holds up a buttercup.

Then she sings this song:

Butterfly, butterfly,
Bright as can be.
Fly, pretty butterfly,
Fly down to me!

Soon the butterfly sees
the buttercup.
Down, down it flies.

Now the butterfly is just
over her head.
She grabs hold of it and...

Whee!
Off they go!

22

At last,
there is the magic garden.
Princess Buttercup is not
lost anymore.

Down, down comes
Princess Buttercup
on the butterfly.

Plop! The butterfly lands on a flower.

Princess Buttercup climbs down.

The Flower Princesses are
happy to see her.
And she is happy to see them.

The party begins.
Everybody has fun.

Even the butterfly!